Kathryn Cave has written fiction and non-fiction
for children of all ages since her first book, *Dragonrise*, was published.
In 1997, *Something Else*, illustrated by Chris Riddell,
won the UNESCO Prize for Children's Literature in the service of tolerance.
Her previous titles for Frances Lincoln include *Just In Time*, illustrated by Terry McKenna
and her collaborations with Oxfam, *W is for World* and *One Child, One Seed*.
Kathryn lives in London.

Chris Riddell was born in Cape Town, South Africa, and studied
illustration at Brighton Polytechnic. He now divides his time between
illustrating children's books and working as a political cartoonist for
The Economist and *The Observer*. His previous titles include *Something Else*,
written by Kathryn Cave, which was shortlisted for the Kate Greenaway Medal
and the Smarties Prize, and *Until I Met Dudley*, written by Roger McGough
and published by Frances Lincoln, which was a runner-up for the
English Association 4-11 Award for best children's picture book.
Chris lives in Brighton.

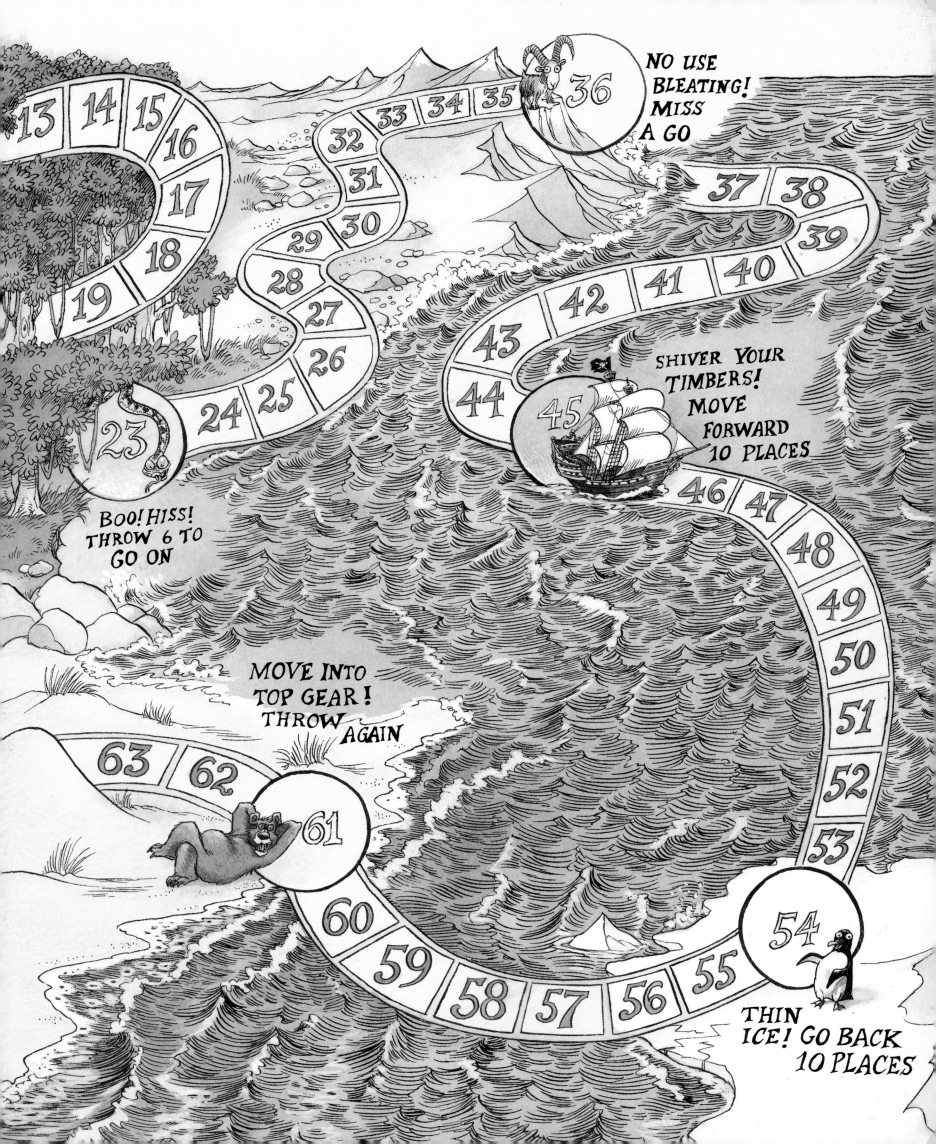

First published in Great Britain in 1991 by
Frances Lincoln Children's Books, 4 Torriano Mews
Torriano Avenue, London NW5 2RZ
www.franceslincoln.com

This paperback edition published in 2006

British Library Cataloguing in Publication Data
available on request

ISBN–10: 1–84507–539–0
ISBN–13: 978–1–84507–539–2

Printed in China

3 5 7 9 8 6 4 2

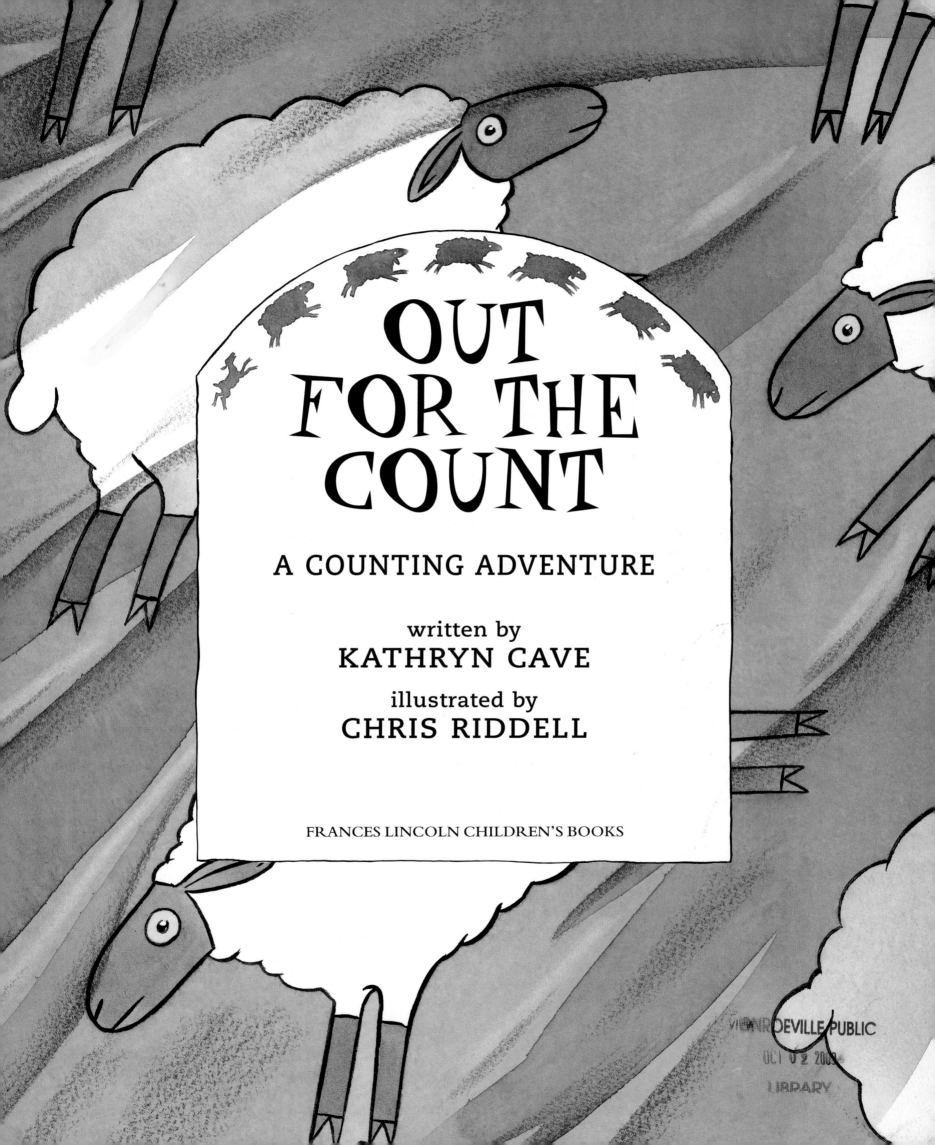

OUT FOR THE COUNT

A COUNTING ADVENTURE

written by
KATHRYN CAVE

illustrated by
CHRIS RIDDELL

FRANCES LINCOLN CHILDREN'S BOOKS

Last thing at night, when Dad goes round
to switch the central heating down
and put the cat out for the night,
all children should be tucked up tight.

One night Tom wasn't: he had had
three drinks of water from his Dad,
six hugs and four good-nights from Mum,
but even so, sleep wouldn't come.

At 10 o'clock his mum said: "Right.
This is your very last good-night.
I'm off to bed. Just go to sleep –
and if you can't, try counting sheep."

Six sheep ambled through Tom's door
and lay down on the bedroom floor.
They sighed and snuffled, yawned a lot,
then fell asleep — but Tom did not.

The seventh sheep was lean and spry.
It looked at Tom and winked an eye.
Before you could say "Mother Hubbard",
it vanished through his bedroom cupboard.

Beyond the cupboard lay a wood,
deep, desperate and dark. Tom stood
astonished till a fearsome growl
warned him wolves were on the prowl.

Two wolves, four wolves, six, eight, ten –
soon Tom had counted 12 of them.
Their teeth were sharp, their manners free.
Tom judged it best to climb a tree.

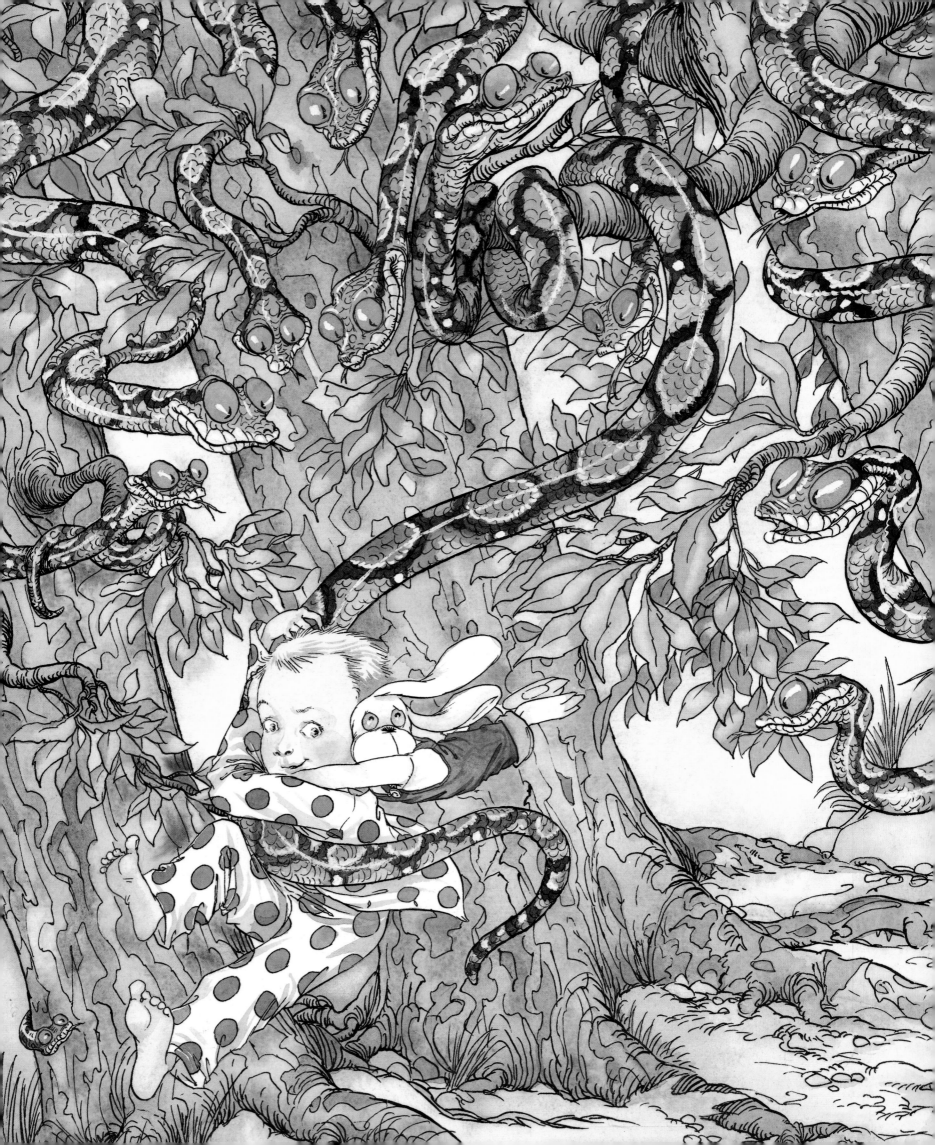

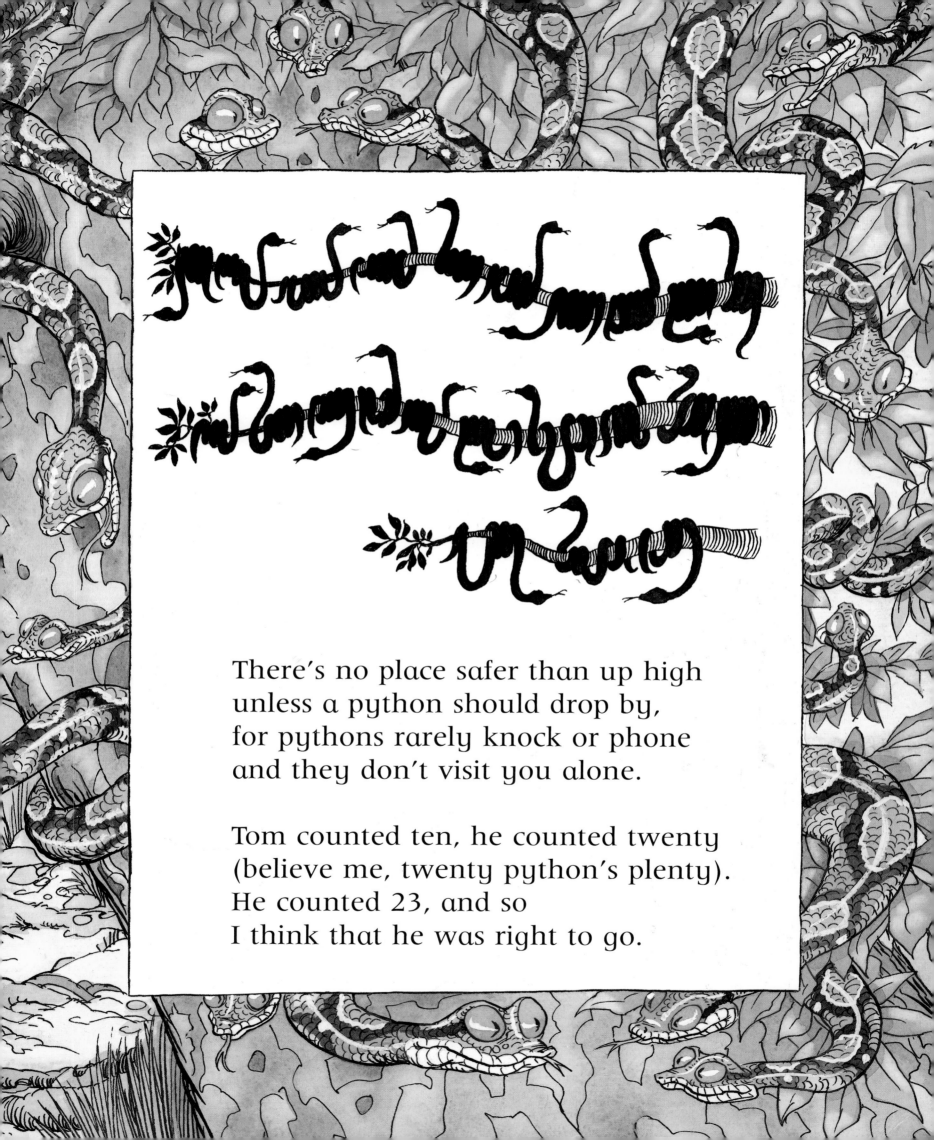

There's no place safer than up high
unless a python should drop by,
for pythons rarely knock or phone
and they don't visit you alone.

Tom counted ten, he counted twenty
(believe me, twenty python's plenty).
He counted 23, and so
I think that he was right to go.

The mountainside was cold and bare.
The wind that whiffled through Tom's hair
brought to his ears a mournful note –
the gentle bleating of a goat.

Some goats are small, some goats are sweet.
Tom's weren't: they had great horns and feet.
When 36 goats cut up rough
one cannot exit fast enough.

Approaching from the east Tom saw
a band of pirates armed for war,
with pistols, cutlasses and axes,
looking for some target practice.

No time to hide, no place to run,
outnumbered 45 to one,
Tom ducked beneath the gangplank fast
and tripped them up as they went past.

The wind grew sharper, Tom grew colder.
Penguins pecked him on the shoulder –
30, 40, 54,
they crowded round to peck some more.

Tom counted west, he counted east.
It didn't change things in the least.
Desperately, as dawn was breaking,
he built an ice raft to escape in.

The beach looked like the perfect spot
for Tom to sunbathe. It was not.
61 enormous bears
seemed to think that it was theirs.

Counting them by twos and fours,
Tom dodged noses, teeth and claws.
I think they only meant to play
but Tom was glad to drive away.

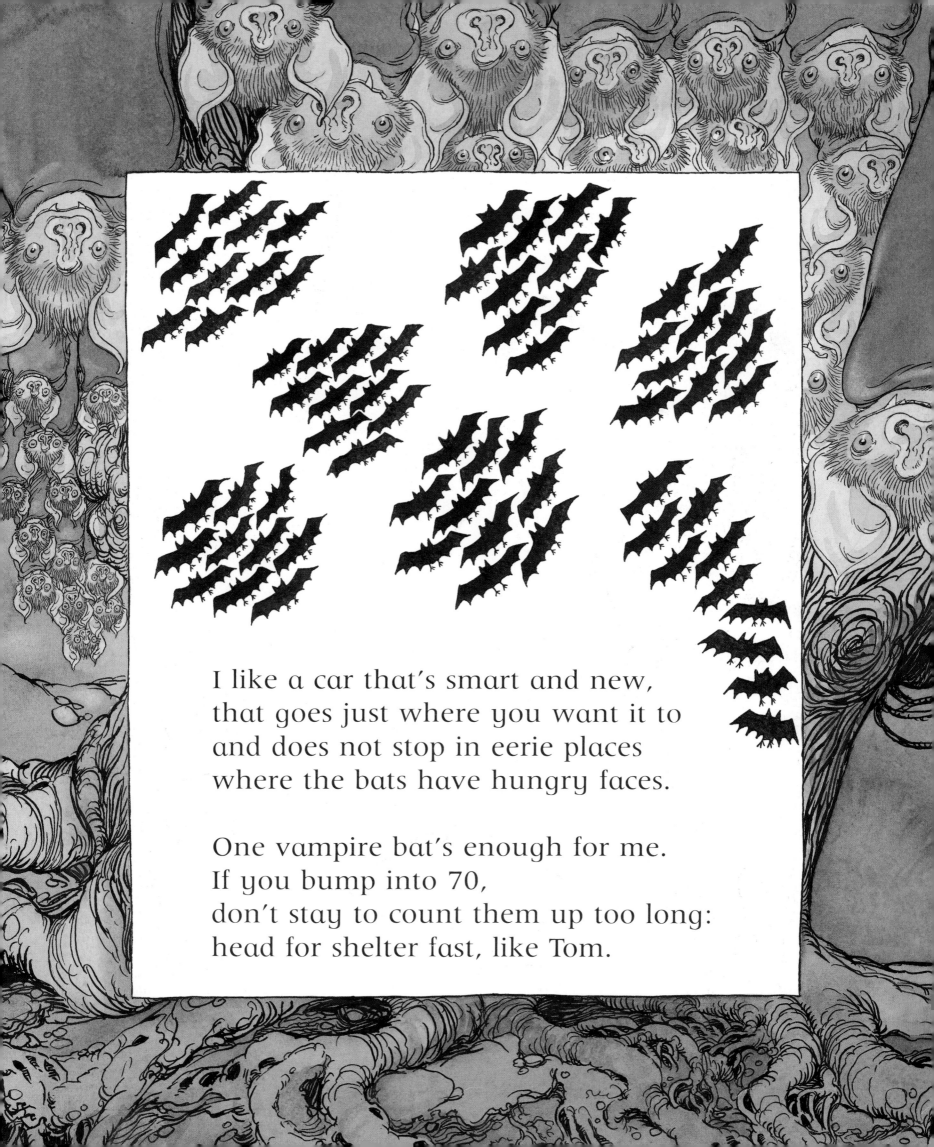

I like a car that's smart and new,
that goes just where you want it to
and does not stop in eerie places
where the bats have hungry faces.

One vampire bat's enough for me.
If you bump into 70,
don't stay to count them up too long:
head for shelter fast, like Tom.

Ghosts are fine in ones or twos,
depending on the sort you choose
(on gloomy Sundays when it's raining
they can be quite entertaining)

but 88 ghosts in a huddle
almost always leads to trouble.
As soon as Tom had finished counting
he dashed out and down the mountain.

Bombay tigers can be kind.
All the same, if you should find
97 in a heap
the best thing is to let them sleep.

And when you're counting them in whispers
please DON'T tread upon their whiskers.
Tigers don't like being woken.
Luckily Tom's door was open . . .

A hundred shadows swoop and fall
across the blankness of Tom's wall.
Tom shut the door, tucked up the sheep,
put out the light, and went to sleep.

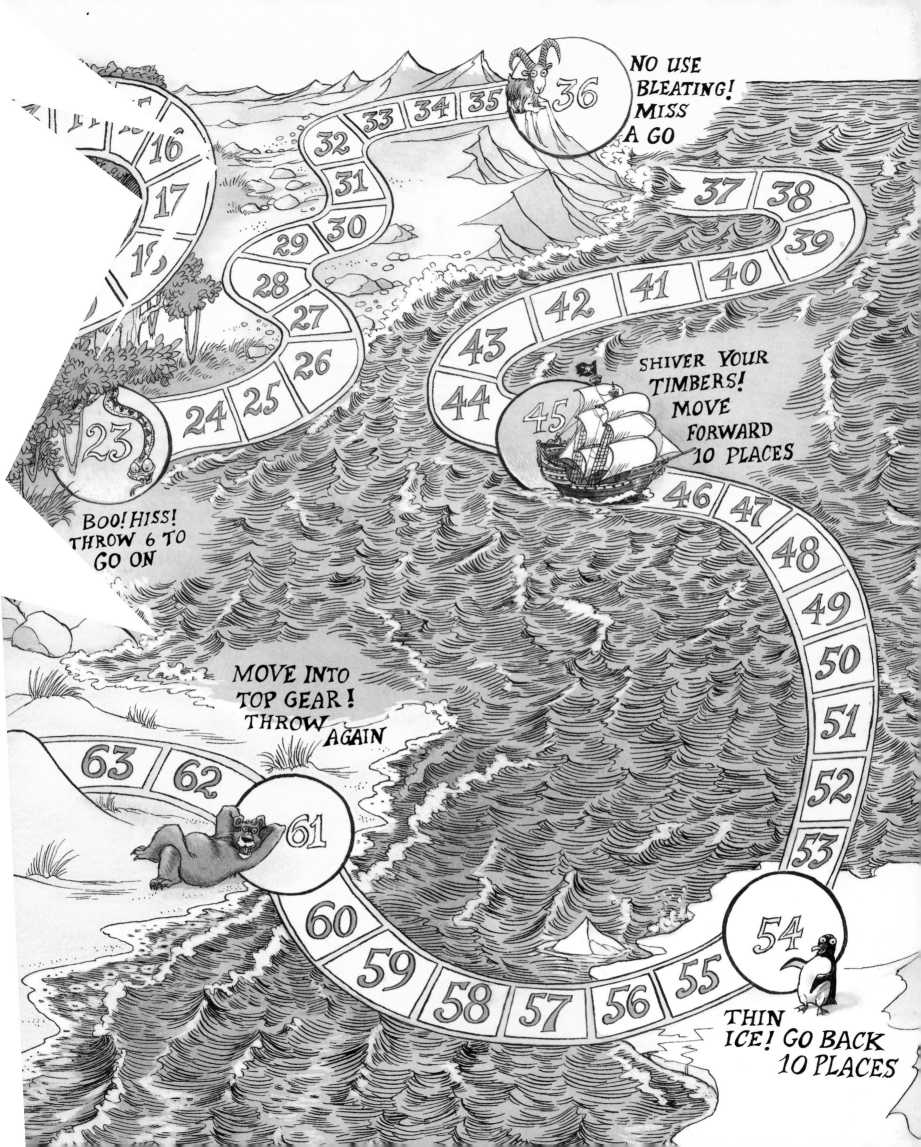

MORE TITLES AVAILABLE FROM
FRANCES LINCOLN CHILDREN'S BOOKS

Until I Met Dudley
Roger McGough
Illustrated by Chris Riddell

Have you ever wondered how a toaster works?
Or what happens to garbage when it's thrown into the garbage truck?
In this fun-filled book of how things work, Dudley, the techno-wizard dog,
takes you through the processes behind familiar machines.

ISBN: 0-7112-1129-9

Number Rhymes to Say and Play!
Opal Dunn
Illustrated by Adriano Gon

Here are 18 lively number rhymes and games to help
your pre-school child develop and extend numeracy skills.
The colourful illustrations reinforce number concepts from 0 to 10
as well as helping to develop language and social skills.

ISBN: 0-7112-2167-7

The Deep Blue Sea
Jakki Wood

Clownfish, flying fish, anchovies, whales – more than 60
remarkable ocean creatures swim, dive and glide through the pages of this
sparkling sea journey. Tom's toy boat drifts on the ocean currents, from California
through the Pacific, on into the Atlantic, all the way to Britain!

ISBN: 1-84507-538-2

Frances Lincoln titles are available from all good bookshops.
You can also buy books and find out more about your favourite titles,
authors and illustrators on our website: www.franceslincoln.com